a country doctor

A COUNTRY

TWISTED SPOON PRESS
Prague

FRANZ KAFKA

DOCTOR

translated by
KEVIN BLAHUT

illustrated by
ZOULFIIA GAZAEVA

ISBN 80-902171-4-1

Contents

THE NEW ADVOCATE

We have a new advocate, Dr. Bucephalus. Little about his appearance recalls the time when he was Alexander of Macedonia's warhorse. However, anyone who is acquainted with the facts notices a few things. Recently I saw how a simple court usher admired the advocate with the expert gaze of an inveterate race-goer as Dr. Bucephalus, raising up his thighs, climbed the marble stairs of the front stairwell with ringing steps.

In general, the members of the bar approve the hiring of Bucephalus. With surprising insight, they say to themselves that, given the contemporary order of society, Bucephalus is in a difficult position, and that therefore, and also because of his importance to world history, he deserves some consideration. Today — no one can deny it — there is no great Alexander. It is true that many people know how to murder; the skill of striking one's friend across the banquet table with a lance is also not lacking; many find Macedonia too confining, and curse Philip, the father — but no one, no one can lead the way to India. Even then the gates of India were unattainable, but the king's sword pointed the way to them. Today the gates are in entirely different places, higher and more remote; no one shows the way; many hold swords, but only in order to wave them, and the gaze that attempts to follow them becomes confused.

Therefore the best thing might be to do as Bucephalus has done and immerse oneself in the law books. Free, his flanks not burdened by the loins of a rider, by a quiet lamp, far from the din of the battle of Issus, he reads and turns the pages of our old books.

A COUNTRY DOCTOR

I was in a difficult situation; an urgent journey lay before me; a gravely sick patient was waiting for me in a village ten miles away; the wide space between us was filled with heavy flurries of snow; I had a carriage, light, with large wheels, just right for our country roads; wrapped in my fur coat, my bag of instruments in my hand, I was standing in the courtyard, ready to go; but the horse was missing, the horse. My own horse had died the previous night from over-exertion in this icy winter; my servant girl was running around the village, trying to borrow a horse; but there was no hope, I knew, and, covered with larger and larger piles of snow, move-ment becoming increasingly difficult, I stood there, without any purpose. The girl appeared at the gate, alone, waved the lantern; of course, who would lend out his horse for such a journey? I walked around the courtyard once more; nothing occurred to me; distracted and tormented, I kicked the flimsy door of the pigstall, which had not been used in years. It opened, clattering open and shut on its hinges. Warmth and the smell of horses emerged from it. Inside, a dim stall-lantern swung from a rope. A man, hunched over in the low shed, showed his open, blue-eyed face. "Should I harness up?" he asked, crawling forward on his hands and knees. I did not know what to say, and bent down to see what else there was in the stall. The servant girl was standing beside me. "One never knows what one has in one's own house," she said, and both of us laughed. "Hey brother, hey sister!" cried the stableboy, and, one after another, two horses appeared, powerful animals with strong flanks, lowering their well-formed heads like camels; they restlessly filled the hole in the door, and, their legs close to their bodies, squeezed their way through it with the sheer force of their writhing torsos. But immediately they were standing upright, high-legged, their bodies thickly steaming. "Help him," I said, and the obedient girl hurried to give the boy the harness for the wagon. But scarcely was she beside him

when the boy seizes her and presses his face to hers. She screams and runs toward me; two rows of red teeth-marks are on her cheek. "You beast," I scream, enraged, "do you want the whip?" but I come to my senses immediately, since he is a stranger, since I don't know where he comes from, and since he is helping me of his own free will when everyone else refuses. As though he could read my thoughts, he is not angered by the threat, but simply turns to me, still occupied with the horses. "Climb in," he says then, and, in fact, everything is ready. I notice that I have never ridden with such a wonderful pair, and am happy as I climb in. "But I will get lost, you don't know how to get there," I say. "Of course," he says, "I'm not going with you, I am staying with Rosa." "No," screams Rosa, and runs into the house with an accurate premonition of the unavoidability of her destiny; I hear the clatter of the doorchain as she secures it; I hear the lock fall into place; I see how she extinguishes all the lights in the corridor, and chasing further on, all the lights in the rooms so that it will be impossible to find her. "You're coming with," I say to the servant, "or I will abandon the journey, urgent as it

12

is. I have no intention of sacrificing the girl to you as a price for the journey." "Off you go!" he says; he claps his hands; the carriage is torn away like wood in a current; I can still hear how the door of my house bursts and splinters under the servant's attack; then my eyes and ears are filled with a buzzing that invades all my senses. But this only lasts for an instant, because, just as though the gate of my courtyard opened directly onto the courtyard of my patient, I am already there; the horses are standing still; the snow has stopped falling; there is moonlight all around; the patient's mother and father rush from the house, their daughter behind them; they practically lift me out of the carriage; I understand none of their confused speech; the air in the patient's room is scarcely breathable; the unattended oven is smoking; I will open the window, but first I want to see the patient. Emaciated, no fever, not cold, not warm, eyes empty, without a shirt, the boy rises beneath the down cover, clings to my throat, and whispers: "Doctor, let me die." I look around me; no one heard him; the parents are standing there, bent forward, silent, awaiting my verdict; the sister has brought a chair for my bag. I open the bag and look through my instruments; the boy continues to reach for me from the bed to remind me of his request; I take a pair of tweezers, examine it in the candlelight and then put it back. "Yes," I think blasphemously, "in such cases the gods lend assistance, provide the necessary horse, and, to make things faster, also provide a second one, in their excessive generosity they add a stableboy —." Only now do I think of Rosa; what will I do, how will I save her, how will I pull her out from under the stableboy, ten miles away from her, uncontrollable horses in front of my carriage? These horses, who have somehow loosened their harness; who, I don't know how, push the windows open from the outside, each sticking his head through a window and regarding the patient, undisturbed by the family's cries. "I am going right back," I think, as if the horses were asking me to go, but I let the sister remove my fur coat; she thinks the heat has dazed me. A glass of rum is prepared for me; the old man touches me on the shoulder; the sacrifice of his treasure justifies this intimacy. I shake my head; I would not feel comfortable in the old man's narrow circle of thought; this is the only reason why I refuse to drink. The mother stands by the bed and beckons me in; I follow and lay my head on the boy's breast; he shudders at the touch of my wet beard while a horse neighs loudly at the ceiling. What I already know is confirmed: the boy is healthy, his circulation is a little bad; his worried mother has filled him up with coffee, but he is healthy; the best thing would be to shove him out of bed. It is not my business to change the world, and I leave him lying there. I am an employee of the local municipality and I do my duty up to a certain point, almost to where it is too much. Even though I am badly paid, I am generous to the poor and am always ready to help them. I still need to take care of Rosa; after that the boy may be right and I will also want to die. What am I doing here in this endless winter! My horse is dead, and there is no one in the village who will lend me his. I have to take my team from a pigstall; if they had not been horses, I would have had to drive with sows. That is how it is. And I nod to the family. They know nothing about this, and if they did, they would not believe it. Writing prescriptions is easy, but making oneself understood by the people is difficult. So, my visit here would be at an end; I have been called upon again unnecessarily; I am used to it; the whole district uses my night-bell to torment me; however, the thought that this time I might also have to sacrifice Rosa, this beautiful girl who has been living in my house for years, and whom I have hardly noticed — this sacrifice is too great, and it takes great subtlety for me to come to terms with it temporarily in my mind and not to abandon this family, who, no matter how good their intentions, cannot return her to me. But when I close my bag and wave for my coat, the family remains standing there, the father sniffing at the rum glass in his hand, the mother, probably disappointed in me — but what do these people expect? — tearfully biting her lips, the sister waving a handkerchief soaked in blood; under these circumstances I am prepared to admit that the boy might in fact be sick. I go to him, and he smiles at me as though I were bringing him the strongest possible soup — now both horses start to neigh; the noise, ordained by higher powers, is probably intended to make the examination easier — and I find: yes the boy is sick. A wound the size of a small plate has opened up in his right side, in the area of the hips. Pink, with many different shades, dark in the depths, becoming lighter at the edges, tender and grainy, with blood gathering unevenly at different points, open like a mine in the light of day. That is how it looks from a distance. When regarded at greater proximity, another difficulty reveals itself. Who could look at it without whistling softly? Worms, as long and thick as my little finger, pink in color and also spattered with blood; anchored in the wound's interior, they turn toward the light with white heads, with many little legs. Poor boy, you are beyond help. I have found your great wound; this flower in your side is killing you. The family is happy; they see me in action; the sister says it to the mother, the mother to the father, the father to a few guests who come through the moonlight from the open door, standing on their tip-toes, balancing with outstretched arms. "Will you save me?" whispers the boy, sobbing, blinded by the life within his wound. That is what people in my region are like, always demanding the impossible of the doctor. They have lost their old beliefs; the priest sits at home and picks apart his vestments, one after another; but the doctor should be capable of anything with his delicate surgeon's hand. As you like: I have not offered myself; I will even allow you to misuse me for holy purposes; can I ask for anything better, an old country doctor, robbed of my servant girl? And they come, the family and the village elders, and undress me; a school choir with a teacher at the front stands before the house and, to an extremely simple melody, sings the following text:

> Take off his clothes, then he will heal,
> And if he doesn't, kill him!
> It's only a doctor, it's only a doctor.

Then I am undressed and I calmly regard the people, my fingers in my beard. I am completely calm, above it all, and this is how I will remain, even though it doesn't help me, because now they take me by the head and by the feet and carry me into the bed. They put me by the wall, by the side with the wound. Then all of them leave the room; the door is closed; the singing voices fall silent; clouds obscure the moon; the covers lie about me warmly; the horses' heads sway in the windows like shadows. "Do you know," I hear, said into my ear, "my faith in you is very limited. You have been shaken off from somewhere, you have not come here on your own two feet. Instead of helping me, you make my deathbed more narrow. I would like more than anything to scratch out your eyes." "You're right," I say, "it's a disgrace. But I am a doctor. What should I do? Believe me, it won't be easy for me either." "Am I supposed to be satisfied with that apology? Well, I suppose I'll have to be. I always have to be satisfied. I came into the world with a beautiful wound; that was the extent of my preparation." "My young friend," I say, "your mistake is that you are too short-sighted. I, who have been in all the rooms of all the patients, far and wide, say to you: your wound is not so bad. Made in a sharp corner with two blows of an axe. Many offer their sides and hardly hear the axe in the forest, to say nothing of their hearing its approach." "Is that really true or are you trying to deceive me in my fever?" "It is really true, take a public health officer's word of honor with you to the other side." And he took it and fell silent. But now it was time to think about my escape. The horses were still standing faithfully in their place. I quickly threw together my clothes, fur coat, and bag; I did not want to waste any time getting dressed; if the horses travelled home as quickly as they had on the way here, I would, in a certain sense, jump right from this bed into my own. Obediently, one of the horses pulled back from the window; I threw the ball of clothes into the carriage; the coat went too far, and hung from a hook by one of its arms. Good enough. I swung myself up onto the horse. The harness trailing loosely, one horse hardly attached to the other, the carriage straying behind, and last of all the fur coat in the snow. "Off we go!" I said, but we did not go very fast; we dragged through the snowy wastes like old men; for a long time the new, but inaccurate, song of the children was audible behind us:

Rejoice, all you patients,
The doctor has lain with you in bed!

I will never get home this way; my flourishing practice is lost; a successor steals from me, but it is no use to him since he cannot replace me; the vile stableboy is raging in my house; Rosa is his victim; I don't want to think about it. Naked, exposed to the frost of this unhappiest of ages, with an earthly wagon, with unearthly horses, I, an old man, cast about. My fur coat is hanging from the back of the wagon, but I can't reach it, and none of my patients, that riffraff, lifts a finger, even though they can move. Betrayed! Betrayed! Having responded to the false sound of the night-bell — it can never be made good.

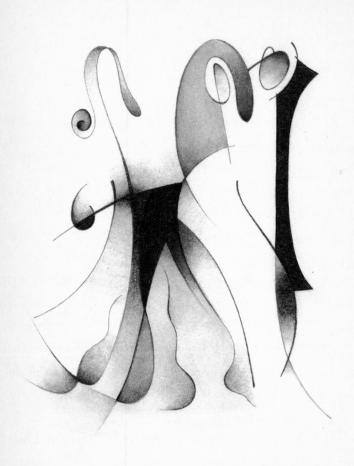

IN THE GALLERY

If some frail, consumptive artistic rider in the ring sat atop a staggering horse before a tireless audience, forced to go in circles for months without interruption by a merciless, whip-swinging ringmaster, flying past on the horse, throwing kisses, swaying from her waist, and if this game continued to the unrelenting roar of the orchestra and the ventilating fans, moving into the gray future that was opening ever wider, accompanied by the fading and rising applause of hands that are actually steam-hammers — maybe then a young spectator in the gallery would run down the stairs, through all the rows of the audience, burst into the ring and, his voice breaking through the fanfares of the orchestra, adapting itself to anything, cry: Stop!

However, since this is not the way things are; a beautiful lady, white and red, flies in between the curtains, which the proud stagehands open for her; the director, devotedly seeking her eyes, breathing at her with the bearing of an animal; carefully lifts her up onto the dappled horse, as though she were, more than anything else, his beloved granddaughter who was setting out on a dangerous journey; cannot decide to give the signal with his whip; finally, overcoming himself, gives it like a shot; runs after the horse with his mouth open; regards the jumps the rider makes with sharp glances; can scarcely comprehend her artistic skill; tries to warn her with exclamations in English; angrily admonishes the stableboys holding the reins to take the most painful care; before the great somersault lifts up his hands to signal to the orchestra that they should be quiet; finally lifts the little one from the trembling horse, kisses her on both cheeks and considers every tribute by the audience to be inadequate; while she, supported by him, high on her tiptoes, dust blowing around her, tries to share her happiness with the entire circus by extending her arms and leaning back her head — since this is how it is, the spectator in the gallery lays his head on the balustrade and, sinking into the final march as into a heavy dream, cries without knowing it.

AN OLD MANUSCRIPT

It seems much has been neglected in the defense of our homeland. Previously, we did not pay much attention to this defense, and simply carried on with our work; recent events, however, have given us cause for concern.

I have a cobbler's shop on the square in front of the imperial palace. Scarcely have I opened my shop at dawn when I see the entrances to all the streets leading into the square occupied by armed men. However, they are not our soldiers, but apparently nomads from the north. In a way that I cannot comprehend, they have penetrated into the capital city, which is very far from the border. In any case, they are here; it seems there are more of them every morning.

In accordance with their nature, they sleep in the open air, for they shun indoor dwellings. To keep busy, they sharpen their swords, fashion heads for their arrows, or engage in exercises on horseback. In the past, this square was always quiet and kept zealously clean, but they have turned it into a real stall. Although we sometimes attempt to venture forth from our shops and clear away at least the worst of the filth, this happens less and less often because the effort is futile and also exposes us to the danger of falling among the savage horses or being wounded by the whips.

It is impossible to speak with the nomads. They do not know our language, and they scarcely have one themselves. Their communication with each other resembles that of jackdaws. One constantly hears this cry of jackdaws. Our institutions and our way of life are just as incomprehensible to them as they are indifferent. Consequently, they refuse to engage in any attempt at communication through gestures. You can dislocate your jaw and twist your hands out of joint, but they have not understood and never will understand. They often make faces; their eyes roll up in their heads and foam pours from their mouths, but they mean neither to say anything nor to frighten people; they do it simply because it is their nature. Whatever they need, they take. One cannot say that they use force. When they reach for something, people stand aside and let them take everything.

They have also taken many good items from my supplies. But I cannot complain when, for example, I see how things are with the butcher across the way. Scarcely has he brought his goods into his shop before the nomads have plundered everything and devoured it. Even their horses eat meat; often a rider lies beside his horse and they feed from the same piece of flesh, one at each end. The butcher is frightened and does not dare to stop providing them with meat. But we understand, and throw some money together to support him. If the nomads did not get any meat, who knows what it might occur to them to do; who knows what it might occur to them to do even if they get meat every day.

Recently it occurred to the butcher that he might at least spare himself the trouble of slaughtering the animals, and one morning he brought the nomads a live ox. He will never be allowed to do this again. I must have lain in my shop for an hour, flat on the floor, covered with a pile of clothes, blankets and cushions so that I might not hear the screams of the ox as the nomads sprang upon it from all sides, tearing pieces from its warm flesh with their teeth. It was quiet for a long time before I dared to go out; they were lying around the remains of the ox, tired, like drinkers around a cask of wine.

It was then that I believed I saw the emperor himself in one of the palace windows; otherwise he never ventures into these exterior rooms, but instead lives in the innermost garden; however, this time, or at least it seemed so to me, he was standing at a window with his head lowered, watching what was going on in front of his castle.

"How will it be in the future?" all of us ask ourselves. "How long will we be able to bear the burden and the torment? The imperial palace has attracted the nomads, but it is incapable of driving them away. The gate remains closed; the guards who always used to march back and forth so solemnly are hiding behind barred windows. The salvation of our homeland has been left to us, the merchants and the craftsmen, but we are not capable of such a task, and have never boasted that we might be capable of it. It is a misunderstanding, and it is killing us."

BEFORE THE LAW

Before the law stands a gatekeeper. A man from the country comes to this gatekeeper and requests admittance into the law. But the gatekeeper says that he cannot grant him admittance right now. The man thinks this over and asks if he will therefore be allowed to enter later. "It is possible," says the gatekeeper, "but not right now." Because the gate to the law is open, as always, and the gatekeeper steps off to the side, the man bends down so that he can see through the gate and into the interior. When the gatekeeper notices this, he laughs and says: "If it tempts you so much, try to enter even though I have forbidden it. But take note: I am powerful. And I am only the lowest of the gatekeepers. From one hall to the next stand gatekeepers, each more powerful than the last. The mere sight of the third is more than even I can bear." The man from the country had not expected such difficulties; after all, he thinks, the law should be accessible to everyone at all times, but when he regards the gatekeeper more closely, and sees his fur coat, his large, pointed nose, and his long, thin, black Tartar beard, he decides that it would be better to wait until he receives permission to enter. The gatekeeper gives him a footstool and lets him sit down beside the door. There he sits for days and years. He tries many times to gain permission to enter, and tires the gatekeeper with his requests. The gatekeeper often conducts short interviews, and asks him about his home and about many other things, but his questions are indifferent, such as important people ask, and in the end he always repeats that he cannot yet allow the man to enter. The man, who has equipped himself with many items for his journey, uses everything, no matter how valuable, to bribe the gatekeeper. The gatekeeper accepts everything, but he also says: "I take it only so you will not believe that you have neglected anything." Over the course of many years the man watches the gatekeeper almost without interruption. He forgets about the other gatekeepers, and this first one seems to

JACKALS AND ARABS

…vere camped in the oasis. My companions were …p. An Arab, tall and white, walked past me; he had …ded to the camels and was now going to bed.

…lay down, my back to the grass; I tried to sleep; I …dn't; in the distance the wailing of jackals; I sat up …n. And what had been so far away was suddenly very …e. A swarm of jackals around me; their dull gold eyes …ing, fading; lean bodies moving nimbly, synchro- …ed, as though responding to a whip.

One of them approached from behind, pushed him- …f through the space under my arm, and pressed …mself close to me as though he needed my warmth. …hen he stepped in front of me and spoke, almost eye …eye with me:

"I am the eldest jackal, far and wide. I am fortunate …at I am still alive to greet you. I had almost given up

34

him to be the only obstacle to admittance into the law. He curses his bad luck, recklessly and loudly during the first few years, but then later, when he begins to grow old, he only grumbles to himself. He becomes childish and, because he has studied the gatekeeper for years and has noticed even the fleas in his fur collar, he asks the fleas to join his cause and change the gatekeeper's mind. Finally his eyesight becomes weaker, and he does not know if the world around him is actually becoming darker or if his eyes are deceiving him. But now in the darkness he clearly recognizes an inextinguishable radiance that breaks from the door of the law. He does not have much longer to live. Before he dies, all the experiences from his time there are unified in his mind to form a single question that he has not yet asked the gatekeeper. He gestures to him, since he can no longer raise his stiffening body. The difference in their heights has changed much to the man's disadvantage, and the gatekeeper has to bend down low. "What do you want to know now?" asks the gatekeeper, "you are insatiable." "Everyone strives for the law," says the man, "why is it that over all these years no one but me has requested

admittance?" The gatekeeper recog
life is over, and, to reach his fading
at him: "No one else could have
here, since this entrance was meant f
I am going to shut it."

We
asle
atte

cou
aga
clo
shi
ni

se
hi
T
t

t

hope; we have been waiting for you for ages. My mother waited and her mother before her and all the mothers before her, back to the mother of all jackals. Believe what I say!"

"I am surprised," I said, and forgot to light the pile of wood that had been laid out to repel the jackals with its smoke, "I am very surprised to hear that. I have come here from the far north only by chance, and am here on a short journey. What is it you jackals want?"

And as though heartened by a response that might have been far too kind, their circle drew tighter around me; all of them had quick, hissing breath.

"We know," began the eldest, "that you come from the north, and it is precisely on this that we base our hope. The north is the home of understanding, and this is not to be found among the Arabs. Not a single spark of understanding can be struck from their cold arrogance. Do you understand? They kill animals to eat them, and they despise carrion."

"Don't talk so loud," I said, "there are some Arabs sleeping nearby."

"You really are a foreigner," said the jackal,

"otherwise you would know that never in the history of the world has a jackal feared an Arab. We should fear them? Isn't it misfortune enough that we are forced to live among them?"

"It could be, it could be," I said, "I make no attempt to judge things that are so remote from my life; it seems to be an ancient conflict; thus it probably lies in the blood; and thus it also might end only in blood."

"You are very clever," said the old jackal; even though they were standing still, all of them began to breathe even more quickly, with agitated lungs; a bitter smell poured from their open snouts; at times I had to clench my teeth to be able to bear it, "you are very clever; what you say corresponds to our ancient teaching. We will take their blood and then the conflict will be at an end."

"Oh!" I said, more rashly than I wanted, "they'll defend themselves; with their rifles they'll shoot you down in packs."

"You misunderstand us," he said, "in the way of men, which exists even in the north. We have no intention of killing them. The Nile would not have enough water to wash us clean if we did. We flee before the mere sight of their living bodies, into fresher air, into the desert. This is why the desert is our home."

And all the jackals around me — in the meantime many more had arrived from far away — lowered their heads between their front legs and rubbed them with their paws; it was as though they wanted to conceal a repulsion so horrible that I wanted nothing more than to jump over them and flee their circle.

"What do you plan to do?" I asked, and tried to rise; but I could not; two young animals had bitten firmly into my jacket and shirt; I had to remain seated. "They are holding your train," the old jackal said seriously, by way of explanation, "a sign of honor." "They should let me go!" I cried, turning first to the old jackal and then to the younger ones. "Of course they will," said the old jackal, "if that is what you desire. However, it will take some time, since, according to custom, they have bitten in deeply, and they must release their teeth slowly. In the meantime, listen to our request." "Your behavior has not made me very receptive to it," I said. "Do not hold our clumsiness against us," he said, and for the first time he began to rely on the whining tone of his natural voice, "we are poor animals, we have only our bite; for everything we want to do, whether good or bad, we have only our bite." "What is it you want?" I asked, only slightly appeased.

"Sir," he cried, and all the jackals began to howl; in the furthest distance it sounded like a melody to me. "Sir, you should end this conflict that tears the world in two. The ancients described the one who would do it, and you are just like him. We must have respite from the Arabs; breathable air; a view of the horizon cleansed of their presence; no scream from a sheep that an Arab has stabbed; all the animals should die peaceful deaths; they should be undisturbed as we drink them dry and purify them to their bones. Purity, we want nothing but purity," — now all of them began to cry, to sob — "how do you bear it in this world, with your noble heart and your sweet innards? Filth to them is white; filth to them is black; their beards are a horror; one must spit when one sees the corners of their eyes; and if they lift their arms, hell yawns from their armpits. Because of this, oh sir, because of this, oh dear sir, with the help of your

him to be the only obstacle to admittance into the law. He curses his bad luck, recklessly and loudly during the first few years, but then later, when he begins to grow old, he only grumbles to himself. He becomes childish and, because he has studied the gatekeeper for years and has noticed even the fleas in his fur collar, he asks the fleas to join his cause and change the gatekeeper's mind. Finally his eyesight becomes weaker, and he does not know if the world around him is actually becoming darker or if his eyes are deceiving him. But now in the darkness he clearly recognizes an inextinguishable radiance that breaks from the door of the law. He does not have much longer to live. Before he dies, all the experiences from his time there are unified in his mind to form a single question that he has not yet asked the gatekeeper. He gestures to him, since he can no longer raise his stiffening body. The difference in their heights has changed much to the man's disadvantage, and the gatekeeper has to bend down low. "What do you want to know now?" asks the gatekeeper, "you are insatiable." "Everyone strives for the law," says the man, "why is it that over all these years no one but me has requested admittance?" The gatekeeper recognizes that the man's life is over, and, to reach his fading hearing, he bellows at him: "No one else could have gained admittance here, since this entrance was meant for you alone. Now I am going to shut it."

JACKALS AND ARABS

We were camped in the oasis. My companions were asleep. An Arab, tall and white, walked past me; he had attended to the camels and was now going to bed.

I lay down, my back to the grass; I tried to sleep; I couldn't; in the distance the wailing of jackals; I sat up again. And what had been so far away was suddenly very close. A swarm of jackals around me; their dull gold eyes shining, fading; lean bodies moving nimbly, synchronized, as though responding to a whip.

One of them approached from behind, pushed himself through the space under my arm, and pressed himself close to me as though he needed my warmth. Then he stepped in front of me and spoke, almost eye to eye with me:

"I am the eldest jackal, far and wide. I am fortunate that I am still alive to greet you. I had almost given up hope; we have been waiting for you for ages. My mother waited and her mother before her and all the mothers before her, back to the mother of all jackals. Believe what I say!"

"I am surprised," I said, and forgot to light the pile of wood that had been laid out to repel the jackals with its smoke, "I am very surprised to hear that. I have come here from the far north only by chance, and am here on a short journey. What is it you jackals want?"

And as though heartened by a response that might have been far too kind, their circle drew tighter around me; all of them had quick, hissing breath.

"We know," began the eldest, "that you come from the north, and it is precisely on this that we base our hope. The north is the home of understanding, and this is not to be found among the Arabs. Not a single spark of understanding can be struck from their cold arrogance. Do you understand? They kill animals to eat them, and they despise carrion."

"Don't talk so loud," I said, "there are some Arabs sleeping nearby."

"You really are a foreigner," said the jackal,

"otherwise you would know that never in the history of the world has a jackal feared an Arab. We should fear them? Isn't it misfortune enough that we are forced to live among them?"

"It could be, it could be," I said, "I make no attempt to judge things that are so remote from my life; it seems to be an ancient conflict; thus it probably lies in the blood; and thus it also might end only in blood."

"You are very clever," said the old jackal; even though they were standing still, all of them began to breathe even more quickly, with agitated lungs; a bitter smell poured from their open snouts; at times I had to clench my teeth to be able to bear it, "you are very clever; what you say corresponds to our ancient teaching. We will take their blood and then the conflict will be at an end."

"Oh!" I said, more rashly than I wanted, "they'll defend themselves; with their rifles they'll shoot you down in packs."

"You misunderstand us," he said, "in the way of men, which exists even in the north. We have no intention of killing them. The Nile would not have enough

36

water to wash us clean if we did. We flee before the mere sight of their living bodies, into fresher air, into the desert. This is why the desert is our home."

And all the jackals around me — in the meantime many more had arrived from far away — lowered their heads between their front legs and rubbed them with their paws; it was as though they wanted to conceal a repulsion so horrible that I wanted nothing more than to jump over them and flee their circle.

"What do you plan to do?" I asked, and tried to rise; but I could not; two young animals had bitten firmly into my jacket and shirt; I had to remain seated. "They are holding your train," the old jackal said seriously, by way of explanation, "a sign of honor." "They should let me go!" I cried, turning first to the old jackal and then to the younger ones. "Of course they will," said the old jackal, "if that is what you desire. However, it will take some time, since, according to custom, they have bitten in deeply, and they must release their teeth slowly. In the meantime, listen to our request." "Your behavior has not made me very receptive to it," I said. "Do not hold our clumsiness against us," he said, and for the first time he began to rely on the whining tone of his natural voice, "we are poor animals, we have only our bite; for everything we want to do, whether good or bad, we have only our bite." "What is it you want?" I asked, only slightly appeased.

"Sir," he cried, and all the jackals began to howl; in the furthest distance it sounded like a melody to me. "Sir, you should end this conflict that tears the world in two. The ancients described the one who would do it, and you are just like him. We must have respite from the Arabs; breathable air; a view of the horizon cleansed of their presence; no scream from a sheep that an Arab has stabbed; all the animals should die peaceful deaths; they should be undisturbed as we drink them dry and purify them to their bones. Purity, we want nothing but purity," — now all of them began to cry, to sob — "how do you bear it in this world, with your noble heart and your sweet innards? Filth to them is white; filth to them is black; their beards are a horror; one must spit when one sees the corners of their eyes; and if they lift their arms, hell yawns from their armpits. Because of this, oh sir, because of this, oh dear sir, with the help of your all-powerful hands, with the help of your all-powerful hands cut their throats with this pair of scissors!" And, in response to a nod of his head, a jackal appeared carrying a pair of small, rust-covered scissors from one of his eye-teeth.

"So now finally the scissors and let that be the end of it!" cried the leader of our caravan, who had snuck up on us from the direction against the wind and was now swinging his enormous whip.

All of them fled with great haste, but they remained at a certain distance, hunched close together, all of the animals so close and rigid that they resembled a narrow hurdle surrounded by wandering fires.

"Now sir, you have also seen and heard this piece of theater," said the Arab, and laughed as jovially as his tribe's reserve permitted. "Then you know what the animals want?" I asked. "Of course, sir" he said, "everyone knows it; as long as there are Arabs, this pair of scissors wanders through the desert, and it will wander with us until the end of time. They are offered to every European so that he might perform the great task; every European is precisely the one they think has been chosen. These animals maintain a senseless hope; fools, they are truly fools. That is why we love them; they are our dogs, much nicer than yours. Now look at this. A camel died in the night, and I have had it brought forth."

Four carriers came and threw the heavy cadaver down in front of us. Scarcely was it lying there when the jackals began to raise a cry. They approached with hesitant, jerky steps, each individual drawn irresistibly, rubbing their bodies against the ground. They had forgotten the Arabs, forgotten their hate; the presence of the reeking corpse obliterated everything, holding them spellbound. One of them was already hanging from the camel's throat, and with his first bite he found the artery. Every muscle in his body jerked and quivered like a raging water pump trying to extinguish a powerful fire, the attempt just as hopeless as it is determined. And instantly all of them lay in a heap around the corpse, engaged in the same task.

Then the leader gave powerful blows with his sharp whip, back and forth through the air above them. They raised their heads, half in stupor and delirium, saw the

Arabs before them; the whips struck their snouts; they leapt back and made a short retreat. But the camel's blood was lying there in pools, reeking; the body had been torn open in several places. They could not resist; they were back again; the leader raised his whip; I seized his arm.

"You are right, sir," he said, "we will leave them to their work; it is time to stop. Now you have seen them. Wonderful animals, don't you think? And how they hate us!"

A VISIT IN A MINE

Today the highest engineers were with us down below. A directive has been issued by the management saying that new tunnels are to be built, and the engineers came to take the preliminary measurements. How young these people are, and at the same time so different! They have all developed without constraints, and their clearly defined natures show themselves freely, even though they are still young.

One of them, black-haired and vivacious, lets his eyes dart over everything.

A second one, with a notebook, writes down observations as he walks, looks around, compares, takes notes.

A third, his hands in the pockets of his coat so that everything about him appears tense, walks erectly, preserving his dignity; his irrepressible, impatient youth shows itself only in his constant biting of his lips.

A fourth makes explanations to the third, even though they are unsolicited; smaller than the other man, he runs beside him like a spirit of temptation and seems to be holding a litany on everything that there is to see here, his index finger waving in the air.

A fifth, perhaps the highest in rank, tolerates no companionship; one moment he is at the front of the procession, the next he is at the back; the others adjust their pace according to his lead; he is pale and weak; responsibility has hollowed out his eyes; he often presses his hand to his head as he considers something.

The sixth and the seventh are slightly hunched over as they walk, their heads close together, arm in arm, in intimate conversation; if we were not obviously here in our workplace, in the deepest tunnels, one might believe that these bony, clean-shaven men with their bulbous noses were young clergymen. The first laughs to himself with a catlike purring; the second, who is also smiling, leads the conversation and gives it a kind of rhythm with his free hand. These two men must be quite sure of their position and, despite their youth, have done great services for our mine; otherwise, how would they be allowed to act like this during such an important inspection, right in front of their director, completely preoccupied with their own affairs, or at the very least, with affairs that have nothing to do with the task at hand? Or could it be that, despite all their laughter and inattention, they are aware of everything that is important? Where such men are concerned, one is hesitant to pronounce a definite judgement.

On the other hand, there is no question that the eighth is incomparably more focused on the present situation than these two, or in fact more than any of the others. He needs to touch everything and strike it with a small hammer that he is constantly withdrawing from his pocket and then replacing. Sometimes, despite his elegant clothes, he kneels down in the dirt and strikes the floor, and then, when he has resumed walking, he will strike the walls or the ceiling above his head. Once he lay down and remained still for a long time; we thought something terrible must have happened; but then he leapt up with a single motion of his slender body. He had simply been performing one of his investigations. We feel that we are familiar with our mine and with its stones, but we cannot understand what this engineer could constantly be investigating in this way.

A ninth pushes a kind of pram in front of him, which contains the measuring instruments. Extremely valuable instruments, wrapped in the softest cotton. Actually, the servant should push this carriage, but it is not entrusted to him; an engineer was required, and apparently he is happy to do the job. He seems to be the youngest, and it is possible that he does not yet understand all of the instruments, but his glance is always fixed on them, and sometimes this almost exposes him to the danger of running the carriage into the wall.

But there is another engineer who walks beside the carriage and prevents this from happening. This man seems to understand the instruments completely, and seems to be their true custodian. From time to time, and without stopping the carriage, he takes a piece of one of the instruments, looks through it, unscrews it or screws it on tighter, shakes it and taps it, holds it to his ear and listens; finally, and usually while the leader of the carriage is standing still, he carefully puts the small object, scarcely visible from a distance, back into the carriage. This engineer is a little dictatorial, but only in the name of the instruments. We should all walk ten paces in front of the carriage and, in response to a silent gesture he makes with his finger, should stand aside, even when there is no place for us to go.

The servant, who has nothing to do, walks behind these two men. In accordance with their great knowledge, the engineers have naturally discarded any trace of arrogance; the servant, however, seems to have taken all of it upon himself. One hand at his back, the other in front stroking his gilded buttons or the fine scarf of his livery coat, he often nods to the left or the right, as though we had greeted him and he were answering, or as though he assumed that we had greeted him and that, from his great height, he is unable to verify it. Of course we do not greet him, but when one regards him, one could almost believe that being an office servant for the mining company is something truly portentous. Although we laugh behind his back, even a crash of thunder could not make him turn around, and we therefore respect him as something incomprehensible.

Not much more will be done today; the interruption was too significant; such a visit takes with it all thoughts of work. It is far too tempting to look into the darkness of the provisional tunnel into which all the men vanished. Besides, our shift will be over soon; we will not be here to see their return.

THE NEXT VILLAGE

My grandfather used to say: "Life is astonishingly short. Now it is so compressed in my memory that I, for example, can hardly understand how a young person can resolve to ride into the next village without being afraid that — completely ignoring unfortunate accidents — the length of a normal life, passed in good fortune, is far from adequate for such a ride."

AN IMPERIAL MESSAGE

The emperor — it is said — has sent a message to you, the wretched subject, the tiny shadow that has retreated before the imperial sun into the remotest distance; to you alone the emperor has sent a message from his death-bed. He had the messenger kneel down beside him, and whispered the message into his ear; the message was so important to him that he had the messenger whisper it back to him. He nodded his head to indicate that what he had heard was correct. And in front of all the people there to witness his death — all the obstructing walls have been torn down and the great men of the empire stand in a circle on the broad, sweeping staircase — in front of all these people he dispatched the messenger. The messenger sets out immediately; a strong, tireless man; extending first one arm and then the other, he creates a path through the crowd; whenever he encounters resistance, he indicates his chest, on which he wears the sign of the sun; he makes progress easily, like no one else. But the crowd is too large; their residences go on and on. If open fields were to spread before him, how he would fly, and soon you would hear the magnificent sound of his fists against your door. But as things are, how futile are his efforts; he is still forcing his way through the chambers of the innermost palace; he will never get beyond them; and even if he were to succeed in this, he would have achieved nothing; he would have to fight his way down the stairs; and if he were to succeed in this, he would have achieved nothing; he would have to cross the courtyards; and then the courtyards of the second palace, which encloses the first; and then more stairs and more courtyards; and then another palace; and so on for millennia; and if he finally were to burst through the outermost door — but it can never be — the capital would lie before him, the center of the earth, overflowing with its dregs. No one can make his way through here, and certainly not with a message from a dead man. — But you sit at your window and dream it to yourself when the evening comes.

A FATHER'S WORRY

Some say that the word Odradek has Slavic roots, and they attempt to prove this with reference to its morphology. Others believe that its roots are German and that Slavic languages have merely influenced it. However, the uncertainty of both interpretations justifies the conclusion that neither is correct, especially since neither provides a way of finding a meaning for the word.

Of course, no one would bother with such studies if there were not actually a creature called Odradek. It looks like a flat, star-shaped spool of thread, and it actually seems to be wrapped in thread, even though these could only be old, broken pieces of the most various types and colors, knotted together and knotted into each other. However, it is not only a spool; a cross-piece comes from the center of the star, and to this piece another is attached at a right angle. With the latter piece on one side and one of the rays of the star on the other, Odradek is able to stand upright, as though on two legs.

One is tempted to believe that this object used to have a form corresponding to some purpose and that it has been broken. This, however, does not seem to be the case; at least there is no evidence of it; there are no additions or breaks that would suggest it; the entirety appears senseless, but also somehow complete. More precise details are not available, since Odradek is extremely agile and cannot be caught.

He resides, at various times, in the loft, on the stairwell, in the corridors, or in the front hall. Sometimes he vanishes for months at a time; during such periods he must have moved on to other houses; but then he invariably returns back to our home. Sometimes, when one steps out the door and he is leaning under the bannister, one would like to speak to him. Of course one does not ask him any difficult questions, but treats him — his diminutive stature alone leads one to this error — like a child. "What's your name?" one asks. "Odradek," he says. "And where do you live?" "No fixed abode," he says, and laughs; it is, however, only a laugh that can be produced without lungs. It sounds almost like the rustling in fallen leaves. With that the conversation is more or less at an end. What is more, sometimes one cannot even get these answers; he is often silent for long periods of time, just like the wood he appears to be.

In vain I ask myself what might become of him. Can he die? Everything that dies formerly had some type of goal and some type of occupation, and in this way it wears itself down; this does not apply to Odradek. Will he therefore tumble down the stairs, trailing pieces of thread before the feet of my children and my grandchildren? He obviously does no one any harm, but I find it almost painful to think that he might outlive me.

ELEVEN SONS

I have eleven sons.

The first is not much to look at, but he is serious and intelligent; nevertheless, even though he is my child and I love him like all the others, I do not have a very high opinion of him. His way of thinking seems too simple to me. He does not look to the left or the right and he does not look into the distance; he constantly runs around in his small circle of thought, or rather, he turns within it.

The second is beautiful, slim, and well-built; to see him in a fencing stance is a true delight. He is also intelligent, but has some experience of the world; he has seen many things, and because of this our home seems to reveal more to him than it does to people who have never left. But this advantage should not be attributed exclusively or even essentially to his having travelled; it comes much more from this child's inimitability, which, for example, is recognized by anyone who would like to imitate one of his dives into the water, which involves many somersaults and at the same time displays a certain wild control. Courage and desire are enough until the imitator reaches the end of the board, but then, instead of jumping, he sits down and raises his arms in apology. — And despite all this (I actually should be happy to have such a child) my relationship to him is not untroubled. His left eye is a little smaller than his right, and often blinks; a small flaw, to be sure, which makes his face look more rakish than it would otherwise; no one would ever criticize this little blinking eye when faced with the unapproachable completeness of his being. I, his father, do it. Of course it is not this minor physical flaw that hurts me, but rather a small irregularity of his character that somehow corresponds to it, some type of stray poison in his blood, some type of inability to round off the structure of his life, which I alone can perceive. However, it is also precisely this that truly makes him my son, since this flaw of his is also the flaw of our entire family; in him it is simply all too visible.

The third son is also beautiful, but it is not the kind of beauty that I like. It is the beauty of a singer: the curved mouth; the dreamy eyes; the head, which needs to have draperies behind it to have an effect; the immoderately swelling breast; the hands, which rise easily and fall again all too easily; the legs, which he moves in a delicate way because they are not capable of carrying anything. What is more, the sound of his voice is not full; for a second it is deceptive, attracts the attention of experts, but then it quickly runs out of breath. — Although, in general, everything tempts me to put this son on display, I prefer to keep him hidden; he does not force his way forward of his own accord, but this is not because he is aware of his flaws, but rather because he is innocent. He also feels like a stranger to these times; as though he belonged to my family, but also to another one that has been lost to him forever; because of this he is often listless and nothing can cheer him.

My fourth son might be the most sociable of them all. A true child of his times, everyone understands him, he stands on common ground with everyone, and everyone is eager to agree with him. Perhaps this universal

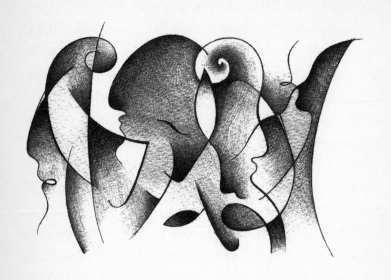

recognition lends his being a certain ease, his movements a certain freedom, his judgements a certain lack of gravity. He says a few things that one would like to repeat often, but only a few, because in his entirety he becomes offensive on account of his all too great ease. He is like someone who jumps up admirably, takes the air like a swallow, but then ends hopelessly, in blighted dust, a nullity. Such thoughts have made the sight of this child a bitter one to me.

The fifth son is kind and good-natured; he promised much less than he delivered; was so insignificant that one felt genuinely alone in his presence; but has turned all of this to his advantage. If someone were to ask me how this came to happen, I would hardly be able to answer. Perhaps innocence forces its way through the raging elements of this world more easily than anything else, and he is innocent. Friendly to everyone. Perhaps all too friendly. I admit: it makes me uneasy when someone praises him to me. It is simply that praise becomes almost too easy when someone praises someone so obviously worthy of praise as my son.

My sixth son seems, at least at first glance, to be the

most profound of all of them. Someone who hangs his head and also talks too much. For this reason it is not easy to cope with him. If he suffers some defeat, he collapses in inconsolable melancholy; if he gains the upper hand, he preserves it by talking. However, I do not deny that he has a certain self-forgetting passion; by the light of day he often fights his way through his thoughts as though in a dream. Without being sick — on the contrary, his health is very good — he sometimes stumbles, especially at twilight, but he needs no help, and does not fall. Perhaps his physical development is responsible for this peculiarity; he is far too large for his age. All in all, this makes him rather ugly, even though some individual parts of his body are strikingly beautiful. His forehead is also rather ugly; there is something shrunken about both his skin and the structure of his bones.

The seventh son belongs to me perhaps more than all the others. The world is incapable of appreciating him; people do not understand his particular type of wit. I do not overestimate him; I know that he is negligible enough; if the world had no other flaws aside from being incapable of appreciating him, it would still be perfect. But within the family I would not want to be without this son. He contributes both disruption and respect for tradition, and, at least in my opinion, he unites them in a faultless whole. However, he knows less than anyone else how to start something with this whole; he will not start the wheel of the future rolling, but the structure of his character is so heartening, so full of hope; I would like him to have children and for these children to have children. Unfortunately, it seems that this wish will not be fulfilled. With a self-satisfaction that I can well understand, which, however, is no less undesirable, and which is also in great contradiction to the judgement of his environment, he walks around alone, without thinking about girls; however, he will never lose his good mood.

My eighth son is my child of pain, and I know no reason for this. He regards me like a stranger, even though I feel a close paternal bond with him. Time has done much to improve the situation; I used to be overcome with trembling whenever I thought of him. He goes his own way; has broken off all contact with me; and, with his hard skull, his small, athletic body — when

61

he was a boy only his legs were weak, but this has probably equaled out — he will probably succeed wherever he desires. Several times I wanted to call him back and ask him how things are for him, why he shuts himself off from his father and what his basic intentions are, but now he is so far along and so much time has passed that things can stay the way they are. I hear that he is the only one of my sons who wears a full beard; of course this cannot look good on such a small man.

My ninth son is very elegant and has a look in his eyes that women find particularly sweet. So sweet that, given the opportunity, he can seduce even me, though I am aware that a wet sponge is all that is necessary to wash away all of this supernatural splendor. But the special thing about this boy is that he has no interest in seduction; he would be happy to spend his life lying on the sofa, wasting his glance on the ceiling, or letting it rest behind his eyelids, which he would like even more. If he is in this position, which is his favorite, he enjoys talking, and he does not speak badly; what he says is clear and concise; but only within narrow limits; if he goes beyond them, which, because of their narrowness, is unavoidable, his speech becomes quite vacuous. One would signal him to stop if one had any hope that his sleep-filled glance would notice it.

My tenth son is considered a dubious character. This is a mistake, but I want neither to deny it nor confirm it. What is certain is that whoever sees him approaching, with a solemnity that is far too great for his years, with a coat that is always buttoned, with an old black hat that has been too carefully cleaned, his chin jutting slightly forward, his eyelids hanging heavily over his eyes, the two fingers he sometimes raises to his mouth — whoever sees him like this thinks: the man is an enormous hypocrite. However, listen to him speak! Reasonably; with deliberation; to the point; responding to questions with vicious alacrity; in astonishing, self-evident and joyful agreement with the world as a whole; an agreement that of necessity tautens his throat and straightens his posture. Many people who consider themselves very clever and because of this, as they said, felt repelled by his exterior, were strongly attracted by what he had to say. However, there are other people who are indifferent to his appearance, but find his speech hypocritical. As his father, I don't want to decide here, but I have to admit that the latter judges of his character deserve more consideration than the former.

My eleventh son is gentle, and is the weakest of my sons; but he is deceptive in his weakness; at times he can be strong and decisive, but even then his weakness is somehow at the root of it. However, it is not a shameful weakness, but rather something that only appears as weakness on the face of this earth of ours. For example, isn't the readiness to flee also weakness, since it is vacillating and uncertainty and wavering? My son shows something of this kind. Of course, such qualities do not make a father happy; they seem in fact to be determined to destroy the family. Sometimes he looks at me as though he would like to say: "I will take you with me, father." Then I think: "You are the last person I would trust." And his glance seems to say in response: "Then let me at least be the last."

Those are my eleven sons.

A FRATRICIDE

It has been proven that the murder occurred in the fol-
ʌwing way:

At nine o'clock on a clear, moonlit night, Schmar,
murderer, arrived at the corner where Wese, the
m, would turn from the street where he had his
onto the street where he lived.

ld night air, sending a shudder through every-
t Schmar was wearing only a thin blue suit, and
t was unbuttoned. He did not feel the cold; he
antly in motion. His weapon, half bayonette,
ɛn knife, was exposed, and he gripped it
examined the knife in the moonlight; the
; not enough for Schmar; he raked it over
that it threw sparks; perhaps he regret-
e up for it, he ran the knife over the sole
violin bow; at the same time, standing

on one leg and bending forward, he listened to the sound of the knife and the sound from the destiny-laden side-street.

Why did Private Pallas, who was watching from his second story window, tolerate all this? Human nature is a mystery! With his collar upturned and his dressing gown covering his broad body, he looked down, shaking his head.

And five buildings further on, on the opposite side of the street, Frau Wese, wearing fox fur over her night-shirt, was looking out the window to see if her husband was on his way home; this evening he was unusually late.

Finally there is the sound of the bell in the clock tower across from Wese's office, too loud for a bell in clocktower; it rings out over the city and up to the s and Wese, the diligent worker, emerges from the bui ing, still out of sight, announced only by the b immediately the pavement is counting his quiet steps

Pallas bends forward; he does not want to miss thing. Frau Wese has been reassured by the sou the bell, and her window creaks shut. Schmar k down; because the rest of his body is covered, he p

only his face and hands against the stones; while everything else freezes, Schmar radiates heat.

Wese stops right on the border that divides the streets, planting his walking stick on the other side. A momentary impulse. The night sky has charmed him with its dark blue and its gold. He regards it unknowingly, and unknowingly he removes his hat and strokes his hair; nothing up above converges to show him the immediate future; everything remains in its senseless, inscrutable place. In and of itself, it is perfectly reasonable for Wese to continue walking, but he walks right into Schmar's knife.

"Wese!" screams Schmar, standing on his tiptoes, his arm extended, the knife pointing sharply down. "Wese! Julia waits in vain!" And Schmar stabs left in the throat and right in the throat and a third time deep in the stomach. Water rats, when slit open, make a sound much like Wese.

"Done," says Schmar, and throws the blade, the superfluous, bloody weight, against the façade of the nearest building. "The ecstasy of murder! Relief, inspiration through the shedding of another's blood! Wese, old night shadow, friend, drinking companion, flows away into the dark earth of the street. Why aren't you just a balloon full of blood, so that I might sit on you and make you disappear altogether? Not everything has been fulfilled, not all dreams of bloodshed have ripened, your heavy remains are lying here, blocking the path. What silent question do you mean to pose?"

Pallas, all the venom in his body raging, is standing between the two front doors of his building, which have been flung open. "Schmar! Schmar! I have seen everything, have overlooked nothing." Pallas and Schmar look each other over. Pallas is satisfied. Schmar continues looking at him.

Frau Wese hurries to the scene with a crowd of people on either side, her face aged with horror. Her fur coat flies open; she falls on top of Wese, her body, clad in a nightshirt, belongs to him; the fur, covering the married couple like the grass on a tomb, belongs to the crowd.

Schmar makes an effort to bite back his revulsion, his mouth pressed to the shoulder of the constable, who light-footedly leads him away.

A DREAM

Josef K. was dreaming:

It was a beautiful day and he wanted to go for a walk. But he had scarcely taken two steps before he was in the cemetery. The paths there were impractical and contrived, but he sailed over them as though following a strong current of water, his bearing unshakable as he floated along. From the distance he noticed a freshly dug mound of earth, and he wanted to stop there. The sight of this mound worked on him almost like an enchantment, and he felt he could not get there quickly enough. But sometimes he could hardly see it; there were flags in the way, and they twisted and struck each other with great force; he could not see the flagbearers, but it was as though a great celebration were going on there.

While he was still looking off into the distance, he

suddenly saw the same mound of earth by the side of the path, already almost behind him. Quickly he jumped into the grass. Because the path beneath his feet raced on, he stumbled and fell to his knees right in front of the mound. Two men were standing behind the grave; between them they held a tombstone; scarcely had K. appeared when they forced the stone into the earth and it stuck there firmly. Immediately thereafter, a third man emerged from the shrubbery, and K. recognized at first sight that he was an artist. He was wearing only pants and a badly buttoned shirt; on his head he wore a velvet cap; in his hand he held an ordinary pencil, and as he approached he began to draw figures in the air.

He applied this pencil to the top of the stone; the stone was very tall, and he did not need to bend down to it, although he did need to lean forward, because the mound of earth over the grave lay between him and the stone, and he did not want to step on it. So he stood on tiptoe and supported himself by holding his left hand against the stone. By means of a very special trick, he was able to use the ordinary pencil to create gold letters; he wrote: "Here lies — " Each letter was clean and beautiful, deeply engraved in pure gold. When he had finished writing these two words, he looked back at K.; K., who was very curious about how the inscription would go on, paid hardly any attention to the man, but instead continued to look at the stone. Then the man was going to write again, but he could not, there was some obstacle, and he lowered his pencil and turned around again to look at K. Now K. looked at the artist and realized that this man was very embarrassed, although he could not say why. All of his former enthusiasm had disappeared. This also made K. embarrassed; they exchanged helpless glances; a horrible misunderstanding was at hand, and neither of them could do anything to diffuse it. At the wrong time, a small bell began to ring from the cemetery chapel, but the artist made a brusque gesture with his raised hand and it stopped. A short time later it began again, but without any demands, and it stopped immediately; it was as though it simply wanted to test its sound. K. was despondent over the artist's situation; he covered his face with his hands and began to sob. The artist waited until K. had regained his composure, and, since he

could find no way out, decided to continue writing. The first mark he made was a great relief to K., but the artist was apparently able to produce it only with the greatest reluctance; the writing was no longer so beautiful; the gold, above all, seemed to be lacking; the line dragged on, pale and uncertain, and the letter was very large. It was a J; it was almost finished when the artist stamped his foot furiously into the mound, causing dirt to fly up into the air. Finally K. understood him; there was no more time to apologize; he dug his fingers into the ground, which offered hardly any resistance; everything seemed to have been prepared; a thin crust of dirt had been put there only for the sake of appearances; right below it there was a deep hole with sheer walls; K. sank into it, and a gentle current turned him onto his back. However, while he was down below, already being taken in by the impenetrable darkness, he watched with his head inclined forward as his name raced over the stone with powerful flourishes.

Enchanted by this sight, he awoke.

A REPORT FOR
AN ACADEMY

Respected gentlemen of the academy!

You have granted me the honor of inviting me to present your academy with a report concerning my former life as an ape.

In this sense I am unfortunately unable to comply with your request. Nearly five years separate me from apehood; a short time, perhaps, when measured with a calendar, but an endlessly long period to gallop through, as I have done, accompanied at times by people, pieces of advice, applause, and orchestral music, but really alone, since all my companions — to remain true to the metaphor — stayed far away from the barrier. This achievement would not have been possible if I had clung stubbornly to my origins, to my memories of youth. Renunciation of stubbornness was the most important rule I imposed upon myself; I, a free ape, submitted myself to this yoke. For this reason, however, my memories became closed to me. Return, if people had permitted it, was first represented by the entire gate that the sky makes over the earth; this gate became narrower and lower as I went on with my forward-whipped development; I began to feel more comfortable in the human world, and more a part of it; the storm that blew from my past became calmer; today it is merely a gust of air that cools my heels; and the hole in the distance, through which this breeze emerges and through which I myself once emerged, has become so small that, even if I had the necessary strength and will-power to run back to it, I would have to scrape the fur from my body trying to get through. Speaking openly, much as I like to use metaphors for such things, speaking openly: your apehood, gentlemen, to the extent that you have something of this sort behind you, cannot be further from you than mine is from me. But it tickles the heels of everyone who walks the earth, from the little chimpanzee to the great Achilles. In the most limited sense, however, I might in fact be able to respond to your inquiry, and am quite happy to do so. The first thing I learned was shaking hands; shaking hands means frankness; today, now that I am standing at the high-point of my career, this first handshake should also be mentioned. My report will not teach the academy anything really new, and will fall far short of what has been requested of me, and what, even with the best intentions, I cannot say — nevertheless, it should indicate the line by which a former ape entered the human world and established himself within it. Of course I would not be able to give even the meager account that follows if I were not completely sure of myself and if my position on the stage of all the great variety theaters of the civilized world were not solidified to the point of unshakeability:

I come from the Gold Coast. As far as my capture is concerned, I must rely upon reports from strangers. A hunting expedition from the firm of Hagenbeck — I have, by the way, since drunk many good bottles of red wine with the director — was lying on the raised hide in the bushes by the water when a pack of us came to drink. They shot at us; I was the only one who was hit;

they got me twice.

Once in the cheek; it was not serious, but it left a large red hairless scar, which is why I was given the name Red Peter, which I find thoroughly repugnant, and which really must have been invented by an ape, since it suggests that only the red spot on my cheek distinguishes me from Peter, a trained ape who died recently and who is known here and there. This by the way.

The second shot hit me below the hip. It was serious, and is the reason why I still have a slight limp. Recently I read an essay by one of the ten thousand windbags who write about me in the newspapers: he claimed that my simian nature has not been completely repressed, and his proof for this was that when people come to visit me I like to take off my pants to show the place where the bullet entered. The fingers of this man's writing hand should be shot off one by one. I — I can take off my pants in front of whomever I like; one will find nothing there but well-tended fur and the scar from a — for a certain purpose let us choose a certain word, which, however, should not be misunderstood — the scar from a criminal shot. Everything is open; nothing is concealed; whenever the truth is at stake, every high-minded person discards the most refined of his manners. If, however, this writer were to take off his pants when people came to visit him, this would have a quite different appearance, and I am willing to consider it a sign of his rationality that he does not do it. But let him keep out of my hair with his easily offended sensibility!

After these shots I awakened — and here my own memories gradually begin — in a cage on the middle deck of the Hagenbeck steamer. It was not a barred cage with four walls; it was more like three walls fastened to a crate, with the crate forming the fourth wall. It was too low to permit standing upright and too narrow to sit down in. Thus I crouched with bent, constantly trembling knees, and, since I probably did not want to see anyone and wanted only to remain in the darkness, I stayed turned toward the crate, the bars of the cage cutting into my back. Such behavior among wild animals during the preliminary stages is considered advantageous, and with regard to my experiences,

I cannot deny that, in the human sense, this actually is the case.

But I did not think of such things at the time. For the first time in my life I had no way out, at least not by going straight ahead; the crate was right in front of me, board firmly placed against board. There was a gap between the boards, which, when I first discovered it, I greeted with the ecstatic howls of incomprehension, but this gap was far too narrow to permit me even sticking my tail through it, and could not be widened, even with all of my simian strength.

People told me later that I made unusually little noise, from which they concluded that I would die soon, or that, should I survive the first critical period, I would be very easy to train. I survived this period. Muffled sobs, the painful search for fleas, the tired licking of a coconut, knocking against the crate with my head, sticking out my tongue whenever someone approached — these were the first occupations of my new life. However, through all this there was a single feeling: no way out. Today I can naturally only approximate that simian feeling with human words, thus causing a distortion, but even though I am no longer capable of reaching the simian truth, there is no doubt that it lies in the direction of my representation.

I had had so many ways out in the past but now I had none. I had been run to earth. My freedom of movement would not have been any less if they had actually nailed me down. Why did they do it? You can scratch all the flesh from the spaces between your toes and you will never find the answer. You can press yourself against the bars of your cage until they almost cut you in two and you will never find the answer. I had no way out, and thus I had to make one for myself, since I could not live without one. Always facing this crate — my death would have been inevitable. But, as far as Hagenbeck is concerned, apes should always be facing the crate — thus I stopped being an ape. A clear, elegant train of thought, which must have been hatched by my stomach, since apes think with their stomachs.

I am afraid that people might not understand my precise meaning when I talk about a way out. I use this phrase in its most ordinary, most complete sense. I intentionally avoid using the word freedom. I do not mean this great feeling of freedom on all sides. Perhaps I was acquainted with it when I was an ape, and I have met people who long for it. However, as far as I am concerned, I did not desire freedom then, nor do I desire it now. By the way: humans deceive themselves with freedom far too often. And just as freedom is counted among the most sublime feelings, the corresponding deception is also among the most sublime. In the variety theaters I have often seen pairs of artists bustling about on their trapezes. They swung, jumped, hung in each others arms; one carried the other by the hair with his teeth. "That too is human freedom," I thought, "self-important movement." What a mockery of the laws of nature! There is not a single building that would be able to withstand the laughter of apedom at such a sight.

No, freedom is not what I wanted. Only a way out; to the left, to the right, or wherever possible; I demanded nothing more, even if the way out were to be a deception; the demand was small, the deception would not be any greater. Make progress, make progress! Just as long as I was not standing there motionless, pressed against the crate with raised arms.

Today it is clear to me: without the greatest inner peace I would never have escaped. It may very well be that I owe everything I have become to the peace that overcame me after my first few days there. And I owe this peace to the people on the ship.

They are good people, despite everything. I still enjoy the recollection of the sound of their heavy steps echoing in my half-sleep. They were in the habit of going about everything with the most extreme languor. If one of them wanted to rub his eyes, he would lift his hand like a heavy weight. Their jokes were crude, but heartfelt. Their laugher was always mixed with a cough that sounded dangerous, but did not really mean anything. In their mouths they always had something to spit, and they didn't care where it landed. They were always complaining that my fleas jumped onto them, but they were never really angry at me because of this; they knew that fleas bred in my fur and that fleas are jumpers, and in this way they reconciled themselves with the problem. When they were not on duty, a few of them sometimes sat in a half-circle around me; they hardly ever spoke, but cooed to each other instead; they

smoked their pipes, stretched out on the crates; slapped their knees whenever I made the slightest motion; now and then one of them would take a stick and tickle me in the place where I liked it. If I were invited today to take a voyage on this ship, I would certainly decline the invitation, but it is equally certain that all the memories I could recall down there in the middle deck would not be unpleasant ones.

The peace I gained while among these people kept me from making any attempt to escape. When I think about it now, it seems to me that I must have at least suspected that I would have to find a way out if I wanted to live, but that this way out could not be achieved through flight. I no longer know if flight would have been possible, but I think so; an ape is always supposed to be capable of flight. The way my teeth are now, I have to be careful even when engaged with ordinary nut-cracking, but back then, over the course of time, I'm fairly certain that I would have been able to bite through the lock on the door. I didn't do it. What would have been gained? I would hardly have been able to stick my head out of the cage before they captured me and put me in an even worse cage; or, unnoticed, I could have fled to the other animals, maybe to the boa constrictors across the way, and breathed my last in their embrace; or maybe I would even have succeeded in reaching the deck and jumping overboard; then I would have floated in the ocean for a while before finally drowning. Acts of desperation. I did not reckon in such human terms, but, under the influence of my environment, it was as though I had reckoned.

I did not reckon, but I observed the situation with great calm. I saw these people walking back and forth before me, always the same faces, the same movements, and it often seemed to me that they were all the same person. This person, or these people, were able to walk unmolested. A lofty goal dawned within me. No one promised me that the bars would be raised if I were to become like these people. Such promises, the fulfillment of the conditions for which seems impossible, are never made. However, if one fulfills the conditions, the promises appear belatedly, and precisely in the place one had formerly sought them in vain. There was nothing about these people that particularly attracted me. If

I were an adherent of the freedom I have already mentioned, I would certainly have chosen the ocean over the way out that offered itself in these people's melancholy gaze. In any case, I observed them for a long time before I ever thought of such things; it was the accumulation of observations that forced me in the direction that I ultimately chose.

It was so easy to imitate people. After the first few days I was already able to spit. Then we would spit in each other's faces; the only difference was that, while I licked my face clean afterwards, they did not. Soon I was also smoking the pipe like an old hand, and when I put my thumb in the bowl, the entire middle deck would shout for joy; still, it was a long time before I understood the difference between a full pipe and an empty one.

My greatest problem was the schnapps bottle. I found the smell painful; I tried to force myself with all my strength, but it was weeks before I finally succeeded. Strangely, people took these inner struggles more seriously than anything else about me. I cannot distinguish the people from one another in my memory, but there was one man who came again and again, alone or with friends, during the day, at night, at all different times; he would put the bottle in front of me and give me lessons. He did not understand me, and wanted to solve the riddle of my being. Slowly, he would uncork the bottle and look at me to see if I had understood; I admit that I always watched with wild, rash attention; no human teacher could ever find such a human student on the face of the earth; after the bottle had been uncorked, he would lift it to his mouth; I watched him the whole time; he nodded his satisfaction with me and raised the bottle to his lips; I, overjoyed by the approach of understanding, scratch myself all over my body, squealing; he is happy, puts the bottle to his lips and takes a drink; I, impatient, desperate to imitate him, soil myself in my cage, which also causes him great satisfaction; and now, extending the bottle in front of him and with the same motion bringing it back to his mouth, he drinks it empty at one go, leaning back with exaggerated pedantry. I, exhausted by a longing that is far too great, can no longer follow him, and cling weakly to the bars of the cage, while he ends the theoretical part of the lesson by grinning and stroking his belly.

Only now does the practical part of the lesson begin. But am I not all too exhausted by the theoretical? Yes, all too exhausted. This is part of my destiny. Nevertheless, as well as I am able, I reach out for the bottle that is offered to me; uncork it, trembling; when this succeeds, I gradually find new strength; I lift the bottle, almost exactly like my teacher; put it to my lips and — and hurl it away with revulsion, with revulsion, even though it is empty and contains only the smell, with revulsion I hurl it to the ground. To my teacher's disappointment, to my own greater disappointment; it is no comfort to either of us that, after I have thrown away the bottle, I remember to rub my belly and grin, even though I do this very well.

All too often, my lessons took this course. And to the honor of my teacher, he was not angry with me; sometimes he did hold his burning pipe to my fur until it began to smoulder in a place I had a hard time reaching, but then he himself would extinguish the fire with his enormous, beneficent hand; he was not angry with me, he understood that we were fighting on the same side against my simian nature, and that my part was the more difficult.

But what a great victory it was for him as well as for me when one evening, in front of a large group of spectators — it might have been a party, a gramophone was playing, an officer was circulating among the people — when, on this evening, unobserved, I took the schnapps bottle that had accidentally been left by my cage, uncorked it in textbook fashion, while the interest of the people there gradually increased, put it to my mouth, and, without hesitation, without removing it, like an expert drinker, with rolling eyes, a gurgling throat, really and truly drank the whole bottle; threw the bottle away, no longer a person in despair, but a true artist; I did forget to rub my stomach; however, because I could not help myself, because something compelled me, because my senses were overcome with intoxication, I called out "Hello!," broke out in human speech, leapt into the human community with this single cry, and its echo: "Listen, he can talk!" felt like a kiss all over my sweat-drenched body.

I repeat: the thought of imitating people held no

attraction for me; I imitated them because I was looking for a way out, and for no other reason. And not much was achieved by this single victory. My voice abandoned me immediately; returning only several months later; my revulsion for the schnapps bottle returned with even greater force. But my direction had been determined once and for all.

When, in Hamburg, I was turned over to the first trainer, I soon recognized the two opportunities that were open to me: the zoo or the variety theater. I did not hesitate. I said to myself: focus all your strength on getting into the variety theater; that is the way out; the zoo is just a new cage; if you wind up there, you are lost.

And I learned, gentlemen. One learns, when one must; one learns when one wants a way out; one learns recklessly. One supervises oneself with the whip; one tears into oneself at the slightest sign of resistance. My simian nature, doing somersaults, raged out of me and away; as a result my first teacher became a little apish, had to abandon the lessons and be brought to a sanitorium. Fortunately, he was released again a short time later.

But I wore out several teachers, in fact a few different teachers at a time. When I had become more confident of my abilities, and the public was following my progress, and my future began to look bright, I found teachers on my own, had them sit in five adjoining rooms and studied with all of them simultaneously, constantly jumping from one room to the next.

This progress! The penetration of the rays of knowledge into my awakening brain from all sides! I do not deny that this made me happy. However, I also confess that I do not overestimate this progress, and did not even do so then, though I think much less of it now. Through an effort that has never since been repeated in this world I attained the education of an average European. This, in and of itself, would mean nothing, but it is significant in that it helped me out of my cage and created a special way out for me, the human way out. There is an excellent German phrase: to slip off into the bushes; this is what I have done, I have slipped off into the bushes. There was no other way for me, considering that freedom was never there for me to choose.

If I take an overview of my development and its goal up to this point, I cannot complain, but neither can I be satisfied. My hands in my pockets, a bottle of wine on my table, I half sit, half lie in the rocking chair and look out the window. If people come to visit, I receive them with all propriety. My impresario sits in the antechamber; if I ring, he comes and listens to what I have to say. In the evening there is almost always a performance, and my successes could not be any greater. When I return home late from the banquets, from scientific societies, from friendly gatherings in people's homes, a small, half-trained female chimpanzee is waiting for me, and, in simian fashion, I enjoy myself with her. During the day I do not want to see her; her gaze has the madness of a confused, half-trained animal; this is something I alone recognize, and I cannot bear it.

Overall I have achieved what I wanted to achieve. Let no one say that it was not worth the effort. As for the rest, I do not want any human to judge me, I only want to disseminate knowledge, I am only giving a report, and to you, respected gentlemen of the academy, I have only given a report.

A Country Doctor
Franz Kafka

originally published in German as *Ein Landarzt*
(Leipzig: Kurt Wolff, 1919)

Translated by Kevin Blahut
Illustrations by Zoulfiia Gazaeva

Set in Janson

Published by Twisted Spoon Press
P.O. Box 21 — Preslova 12
150 21 Prague 5, Czech Republic
info@twistedspoon.com
www.twistedspoon.com

Printed in the Czech Republic

Distributed to the trade in North America by

SCB DISTRIBUTORS
15608 South New Century Drive
Gardena, CA 90248-2129
toll free: 1-800-729-6423
info@scbdistributors.com
www.scbdistributors.com

10 9 8 7 6 5 4 3 2